Series 401
A Ladybird Book

GINGER'S ADVENTURES *is an exciting story in verse suitable for telling to the very young child.*

The full-page colour illustrations by A. J. MacGregor reach a high standard of excellence and will make an instant appeal to all children.

For a list of the companion titles in this attractive series see the back of this book.

© LADYBIRD BOOKS LTD MCMXLII

All rights reserved. No part of this publication may be reproduced, stored in a retrieval system, or transmitted in any form or by any means, electronic, mechanical, photo-copying, recording or otherwise, without the prior consent of the copyright owner.

GINGER'S ADVENTURES

Story and illustrations by
A. J. MACGREGOR

Revised verses by
W. PERRING

Ladybird Books Loughborough

Ginger's bedroom was a kennel
In the garden by the wall,
Where he often lay a-dozing,
Waiting for his friend to call.

Little Tommy, Ginger's neighbour,
Called for Ginger every day:
Took him out in wind and sunshine,
Out across the farm to play.

Once, when Tommy didn't fetch him,
    Ginger turned his little head,
Saw his mother wasn't looking,
    Said, "I'll visit Tom, instead!"

Ginger saw the Quackies swimming

On his way across the farm:

Ran along beside them barking,

Filled the Quackies with alarm!

Tommy heard, and came and tied him,
Saying, "That's a naughty game,
Ginger mustn't bark at Quackies!"
Ginger hung his head in shame.

Tommy, sorry, fetched a basin
 Full of milk, said " Never mind."
Ginger loved him for his goodness,
 . . . Tom was always very kind.

One sad day, there came a parting:
    Ginger was to go away,
Right away to live in London,
    No more on the farm to play.

Heavy-hearted, Tommy whispered,
    "Goodbye, Ginger! Here's a bone!"
Off went Ginger to the station;
    Tom was left behind alone.

Ginger, lonely in the cage-box,
　　Trembled as the train began:
Lay there whining, broken-hearted,
　　In the gloomy luggage-van.

Sorrowfully, in the garden,

    Tommy waved a last " Goodbye ! "

To the train upon its journey,

    Clanking as it puffered by.

Up in London, on the platform,

    Joan was waiting, dressed in red:

Heard him whining, came and found him.

    "Hello, Ginger dear!" she said.

Then she fastened on the collar,

    Took him out along the street.

Ginger found it very different,

    Thought, "What funny dogs to meet!"

Ginger found his life in London
  Very dull and much too good.
Sitting on a silken cushion,
  Like a little dog of wood!

Ginger, looking round for mischief,
    Found Angelica one day,
Sitting quiet in a bedroom,
    Thought he'd take her out to play.

Took her by the arm and pulled her,
　　Down slid dolly to the floor:
Then a sudden sound alarmed him!
　　Joan stood staring at the door!

Joan was very, very angry!
　　Ginger thought he'd better go!
Dashing swiftly through the doorway,
　　Ginger darted down below!

Poor Angelica was carried,

    Tumble-bumping down the stair,

Lost an arm, and, in the scramble,

    Ginger left her lying there!

Dashed by Mary, busy scrubbing,

By the bucket in the hall,

Mary screamed, the pail went over!

Ginger didn't care at all!

Out he scampered through the garden,

Breaking flowers in his flight,

While the angry cries behind him

Only added to his fright!

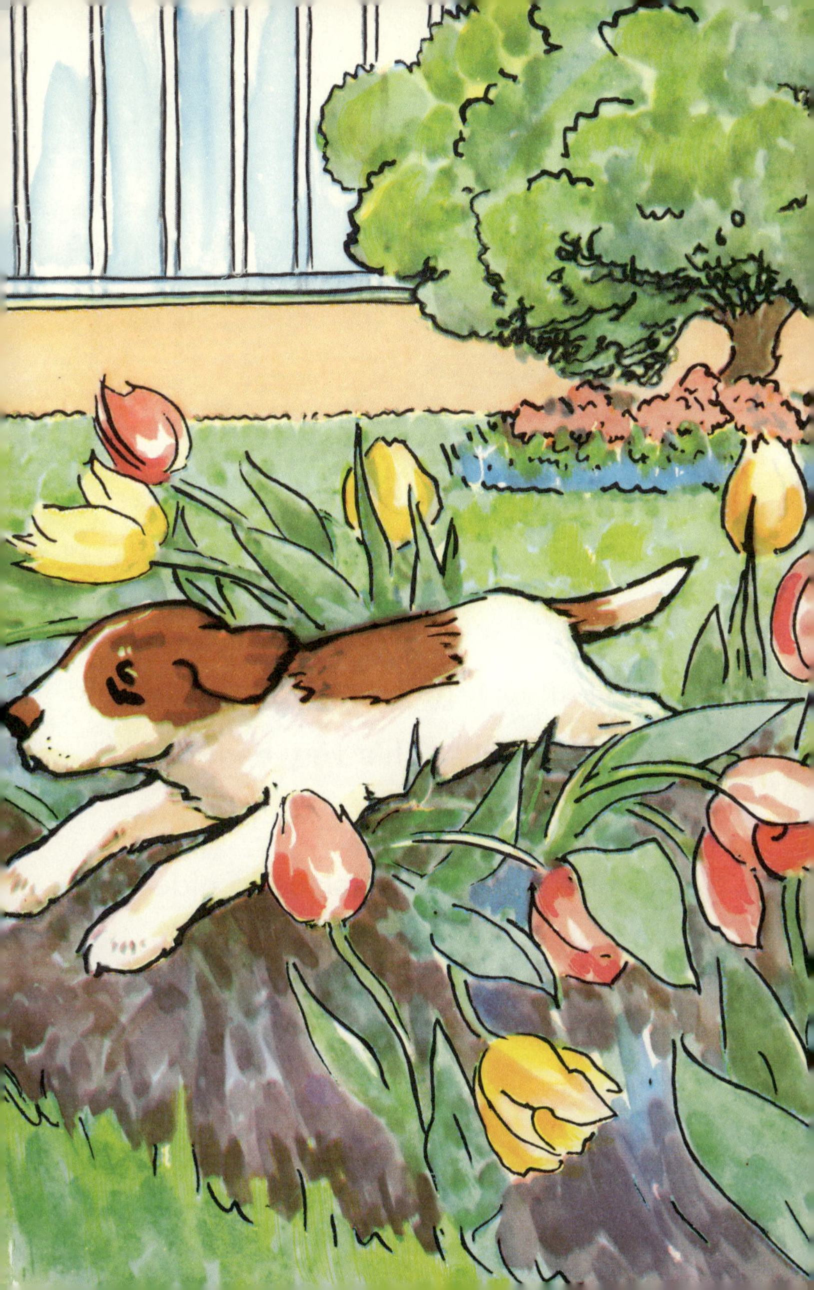

Till, at last, he reached the tool-shed,
Thought, "It's very dark inside!
Joan and Mary wouldn't find me,
It's a splendid place to hide!"

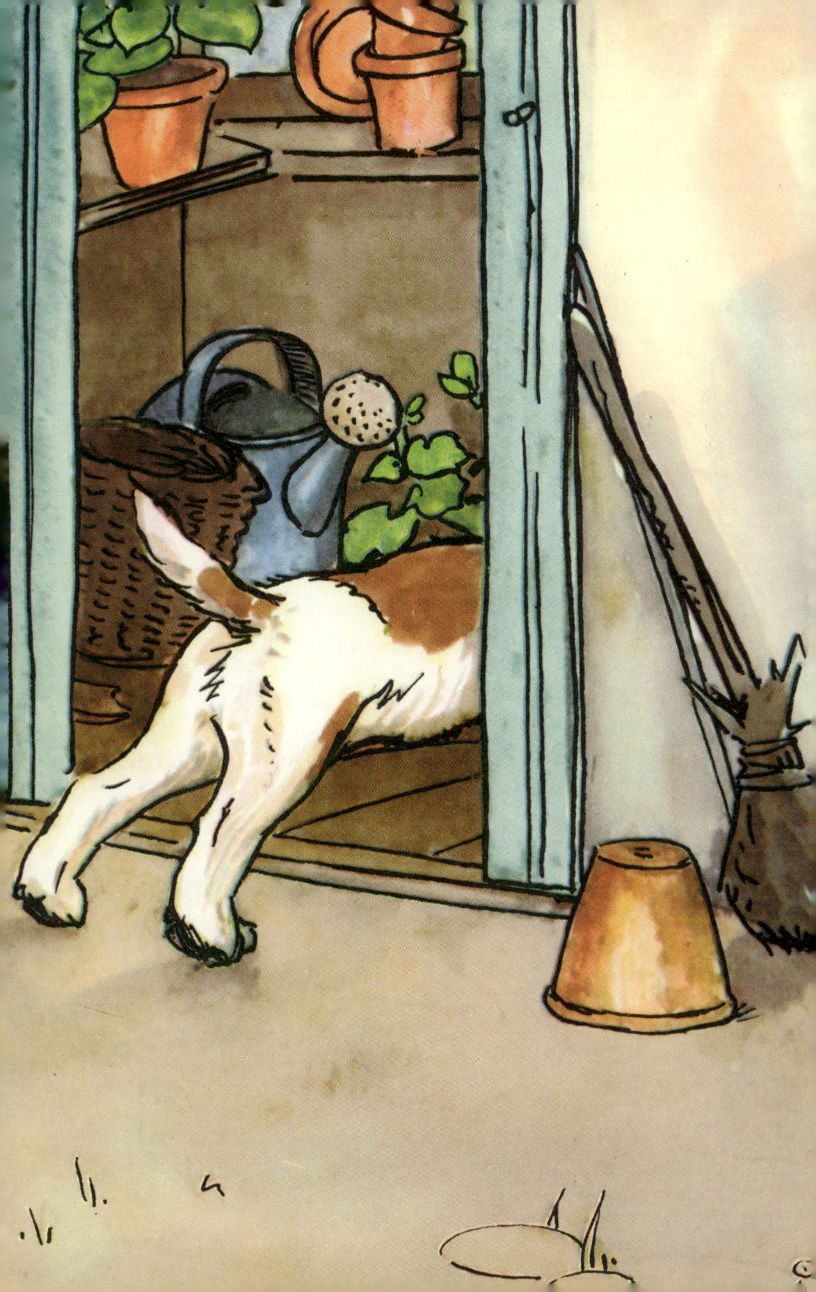

So he crawled inside a basket,

    Shivered, thought of his disgrace.

Mary came! Alas! for Ginger!

    She had guessed the very place!

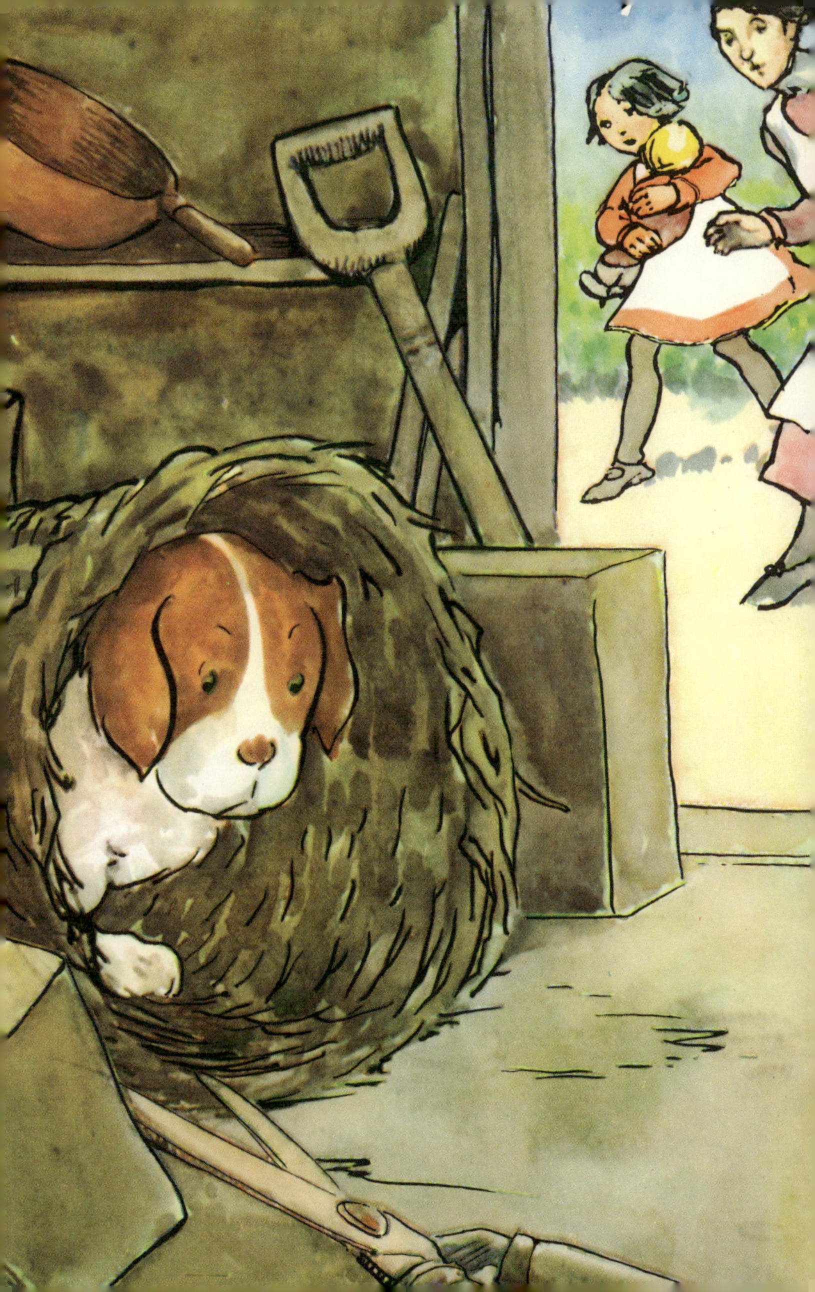

Mary took him from the basket,

    Saying sternly, " Come with me ! "

Dropped him in a box, and added,

    " Stay in there, till after tea ! "

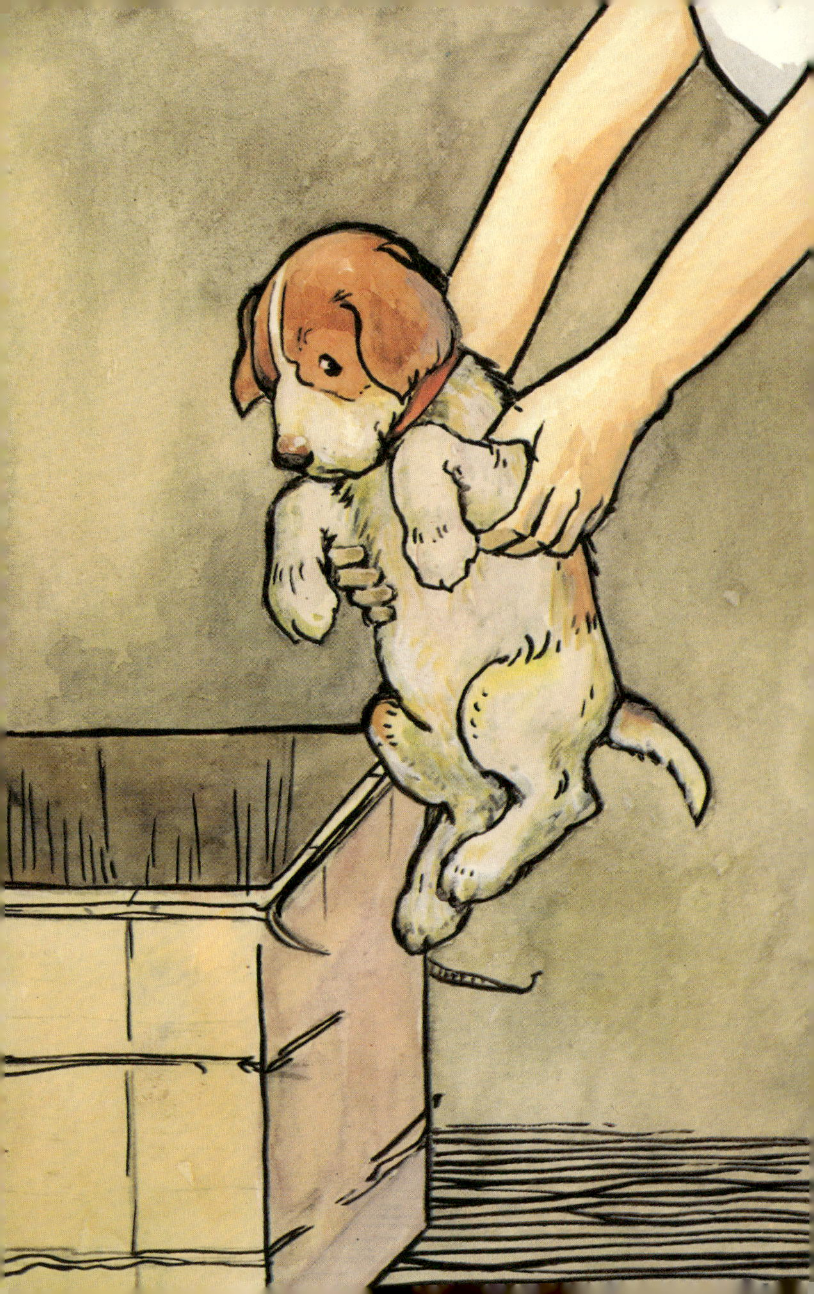

Ginger longed for little Tommy,

    Longed for days that used to be,

When there were no dolls and cushions,

    When the hours were glad and free.

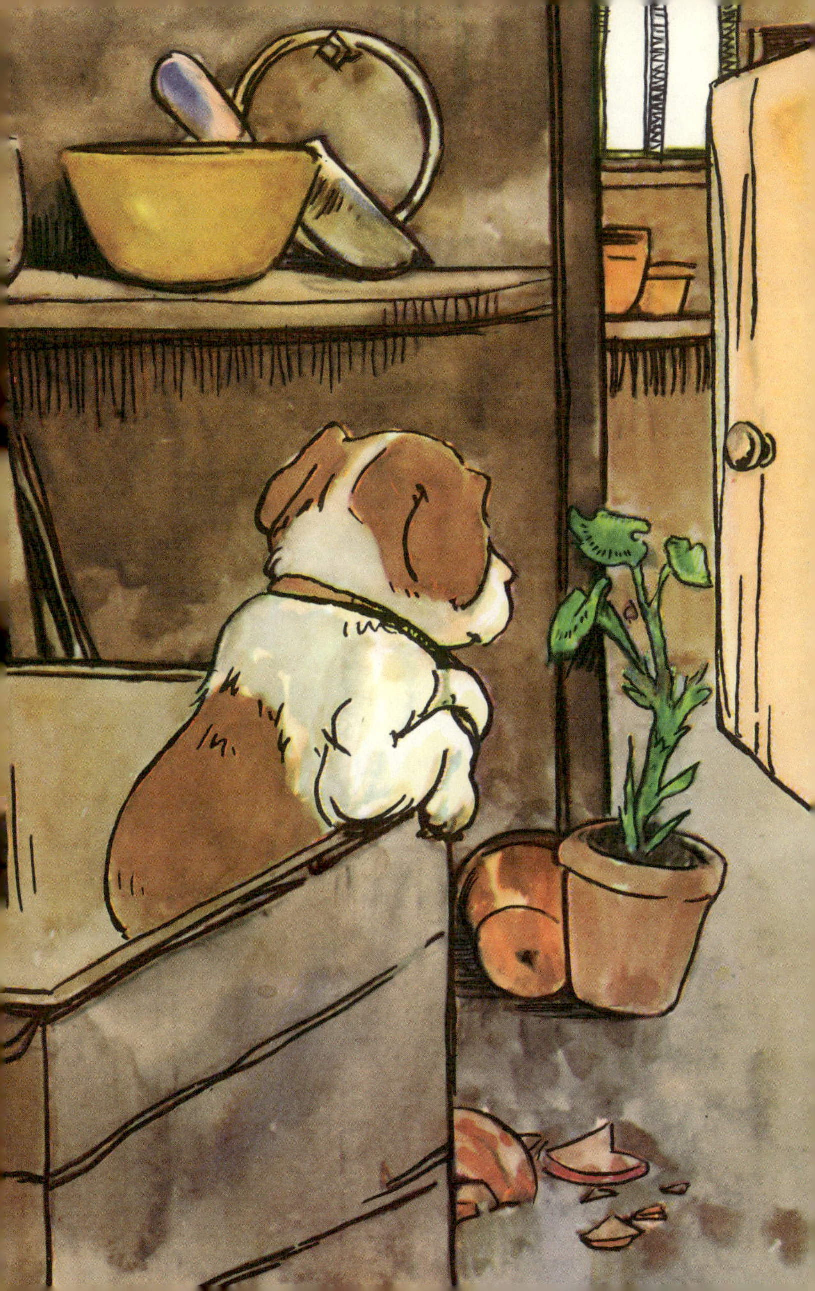

Then the great idea struck him,

    Then he made his splendid plan!

"I'll escape and go to Tommy!"

    Out he leapt and off he ran!

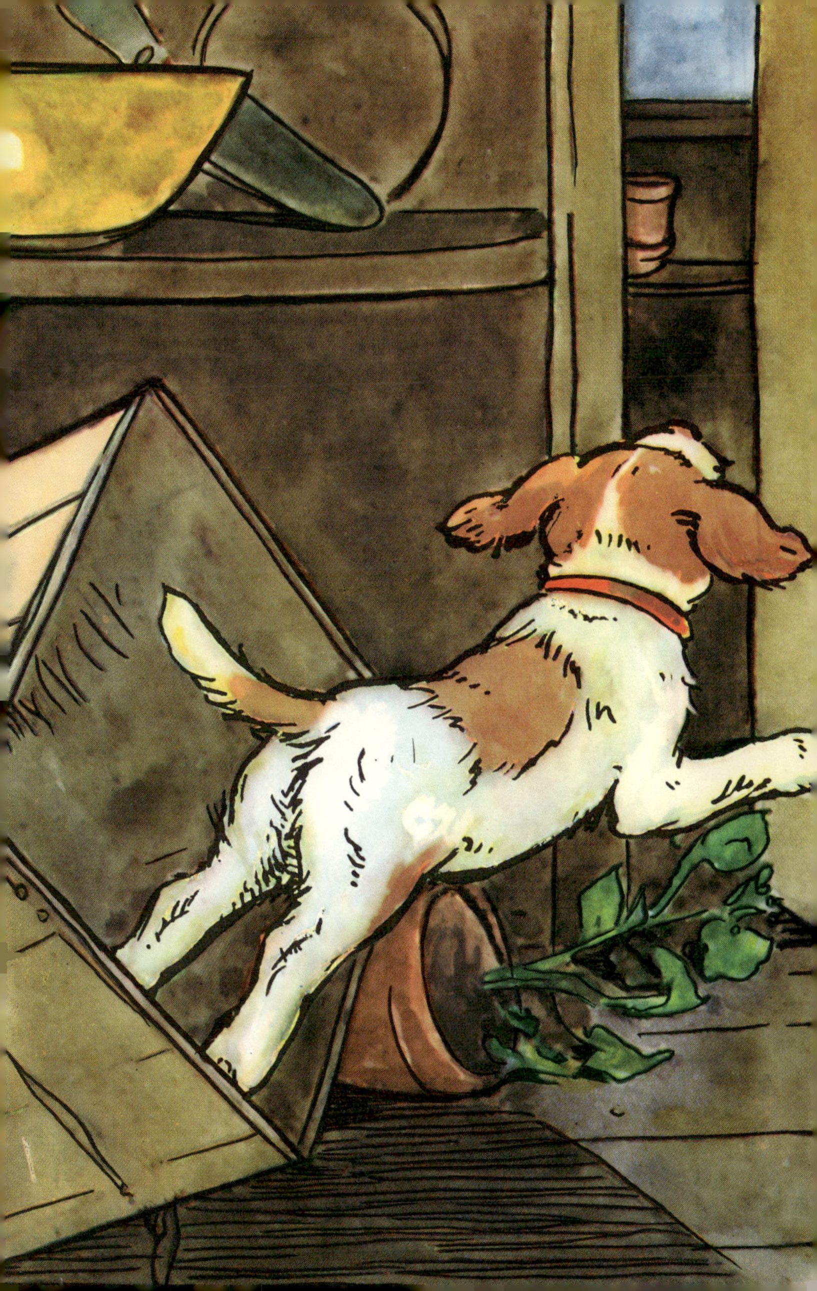

Through the garden, through the railings,
　　Out into the busy street,
Through the city, through the country,
　　Onward went his flying feet!

So, at last, came happy Ginger
    Down the well-remembered lane,
To the farm-house: Tommy hugged him,
    "You shall never go again!"

So the friends remained together,
    Friends for ever and a day,
Going out, in wind and sunshine,
    Out across the farm to play.

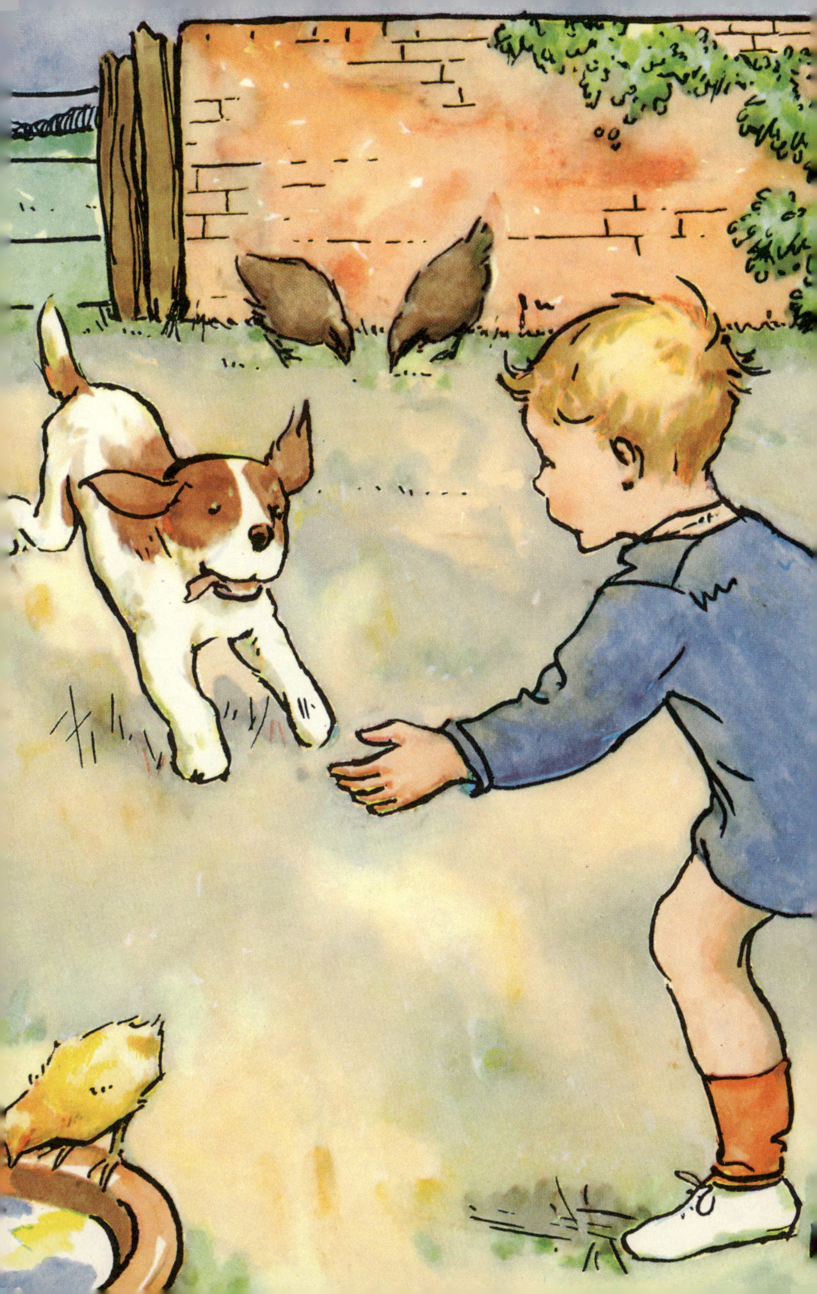

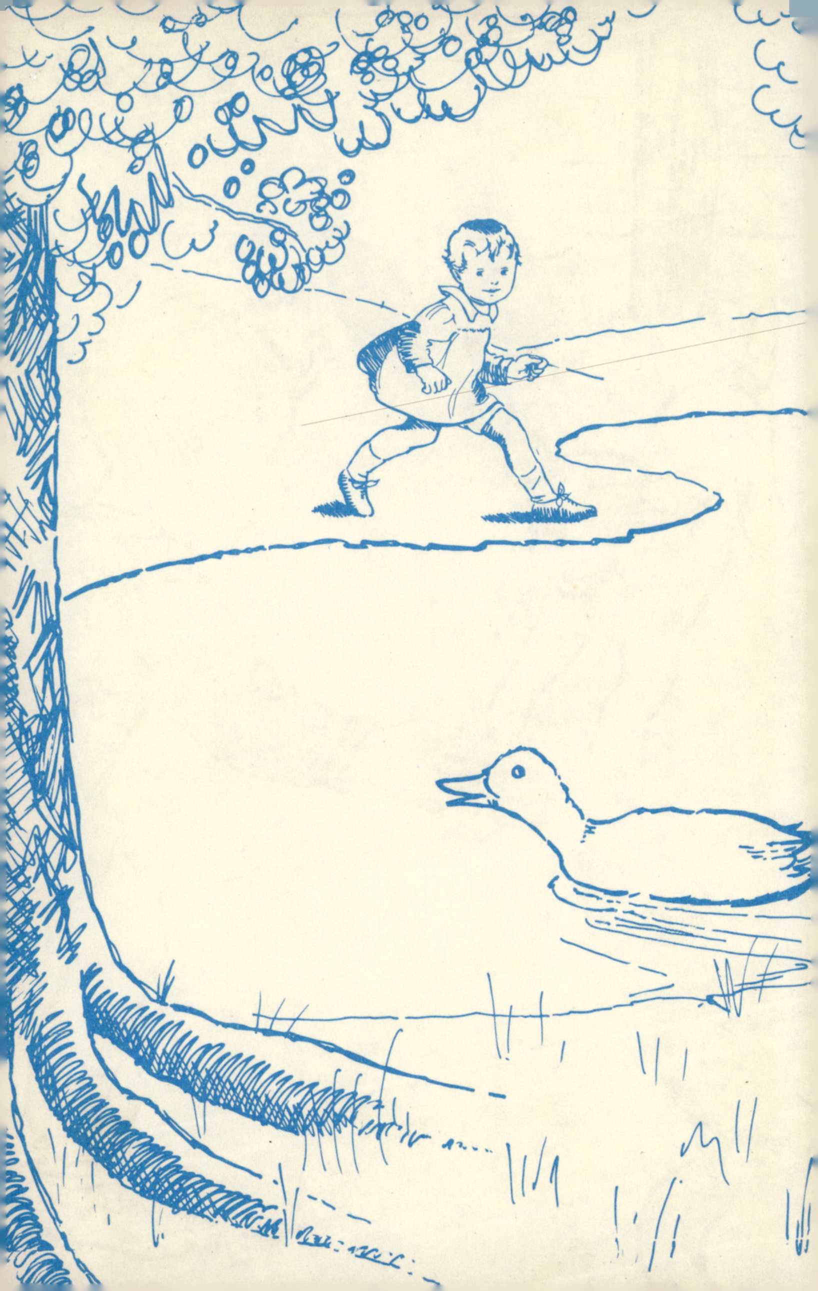